To Joshua and Bethany (who always starts a hug!)
M.C.

To my family and Sam
V.B.

This edition published by Parragon in 2012
Parragon
Chartist House
15–17 Trim Street
Bath BA1 1HA, UK
www.parragon.com

Published by arrangement with Meadowside Children's Books
185 Fleet Street, London, EC4A 2HS

Text © Michael Catchpool 2008
Illustrations © Victoria Ball 2008

Printed in China

That Yucky Love Thing

Michael Catchpool • Victoria Ball

Bath • New York • Singapore • Hong Kong • Cologne • Delhi
Melbourne • Amsterdam • Johannesburg • Shenzhen

Sam was fed up. There was too much of **that yucky love thing** around for his liking. Wherever he turned it was there. His mom and his dad were always hugging…

Yuck!

And kissing… Yuck!

His grandparents were even worse...

Double Yuck!

His sister was no better. She was always holding hands with her boyfriend Wayne . . . or Scott . . . or Matthew.

Yuck . . .   Yuck . . .   Yuck!

Or listening to songs about love . . . Or sighing about it . . . Or giggling about it . . . Sometimes she even cried about it with her friend Emily.

Double Yuck!

Sam had had enough. He needed to escape.
'That yucky love thing, it's not for me!' he said.
So he got on his bike and rode away. He pedalled
and pedalled, until he came to a . . .

deep, dark
jungle.

But that was no better...

it was even worse!
The monkeys swung through
the trees arm in arm...

Yuck!

The elephants
gave each other long,
wet kisses, with their
long, wet trunks...

Yuck!

And the bears
spent all day hugging...

Double *Yuck!*

'I can't stand it!
**This yucky love thing,
it's not for me!**'
Sam told a tiger as he got on
his bike and rode away.

Sam went to the bottom of the sea in a submarine he borrowed from an old sailor who was practicing his trumpet. But that was no better...

it was worse!

The dolphins blew heart-shaped bubbles at each other... *Yuck!*

The big, blue whales gave each other big, blue kisses with their big, blue lips (and there's nothing quite as big as a big, blue whale kiss!)...

Yuck!

Even the crabs spent all day holding claws.

Double **Yuck!**

'I can't stand it!' said Sam. 'I must get away,
this yucky love thing, it's not for me!'

So Sam went to the moon in a rocket of his own design. But that was no better . . .

it was worse, **much worse.**

Down in the craters, behind the moon rocks, the moon aliens were all holding hands . . . and they had a lot of hands . . . *Yuck!*

And kissing – they had a lot of lips too . . .

Yuck, yuck, yuck, YUCK!

Sam got into a boat and set sail.
He found himself on a tiny island all alone.
He sat under a palm tree in the shade.

'That's better,' he said, 'now I'm all
alone there won't be any more of

that yucky love thing!'

Sam gathered shells on his own. He lined
them up on the sand and watched the
sea wash all around them.

Sam scrambled over the
slippery rocks and popped
seaweed on his own.

He even jumped over the
waves all by himself, his toes
sinking in the wet sand.

'That's better,' he said quietly, but there was no one there to hear him. So Sam watched the sun go down on his island...

all by himself.

When the sun rose, a big shadow appeared.
Someone was standing over him.
'Who are you?' asked Sam, 'and what are you doing on my island?'
'I'm Samantha and this is my island.'
'No it's not, it's mine,' said Sam. 'I've come here
to get away from all **that yucky love thing.**'
'So have I,' laughed Samantha.

'It's *yucky*, isn't it?'

'Double Yucky!' said Sam.

'There's too much of it for my liking!'
'And mine!' said Samantha.

So Sam and Samantha
spent all day getting right
away from it. They collected
shells together . . .

They jumped
over waves . . .

They even
clambered over the
slippery rocks . . .

until Sam

slipped,

and tripped

and fell.

'Got you,' said Samantha,
catching him by the hand.

'Thank you,' said Sam.
'You're welcome,' replied Samantha and
she gave his hand a little squeeze.

Then Sam and Samantha . . .

...held hands

all the way along the beach.

'Yuck!' said Sam.

'Double Yuck!' laughed Samantha.